3-8

Published in the United States of America by
Abingdon Press, 201 Eighth Avenue South, Nashville, Tennessee 37202
ISBN 0-687-49719-1

First edition 2006

Copyright © 2005 Anno Domini Publishing
1 Churchgates, The Wilderness, Berkhamsted, Herts HP4 2UB, England
Text copyright © 2005 Anno Domini Publishing, Stephanie Jeffs
Illustrations copyright © 2005 Jacqui Thomas

Editorial Director Annette Reynolds
Editor Nicola Bull
Art Director Gerald Rogers
Pre-production Krystyna Kowalska Hewitt
Production John Laister

Printed and bound in Singapore

JOSH

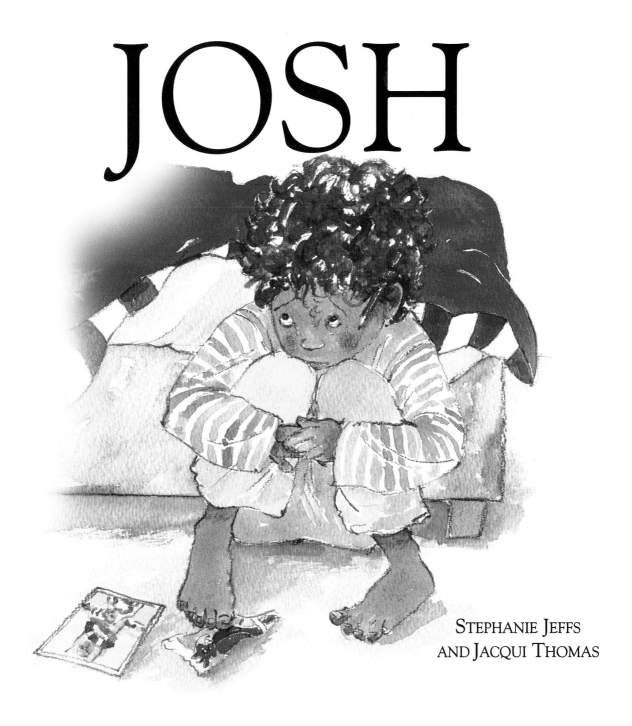

STEPHANIE JEFFS
AND JACQUI THOMAS

Josh and his big sister, Jane, walked past Max's house every day.

Sometimes they saw him through the window. Max always waved.

Sometimes they saw him working in the garden. He loved gardening. In the summer he often gave Josh and Jane an apple from his tree.

Sometimes they saw him pushing his baby daughter on the swing, or playing with his dog.

Max always smiled and waved and said, "Hello!"

Last year, Mom had asked Max to come and decorate Josh's bedroom.

They had chosen the yellow paint together. They had looked at different wallpaper, until at last they had chosen the paper with bright parrots all around it.

When it was finished, Max thought the room looked brilliant. Josh thought so too.

Mom had taken a photograph of Max and Josh, standing by the ladder.

10

Sometimes Josh pretended he was Max. He put a pencil behind his ear and tried to whistle.

Josh wanted to be just like Max when he grew up.

11

Sometimes, Josh and Jane would see Max load his ladders and paint brushes on to his van. Josh liked to see the van, with its big sign on the side.

"Cheerio!" called Max, as he drove away from his house.

The children waved. They didn't know anyone else who said, "Cheerio!" They didn't know anyone else like Max. They liked him very much.

13

But one day Josh and Jane walked past Max's house and they did not see him.

They couldn't see him through the window, and they couldn't see him in the garden. His van wasn't parked outside his house, and the apples lay on the ground.

"Where's Max?" asked Josh when he got home. "Where's Max gone, Mom?"

Josh's mom held his hand.

"Josh," she said, "something very sad has happened. Max has been in an accident. He died early yesterday morning."

"Oh," said Josh, and switched on the television.

Later Josh lay on his bed. He didn't want to play. He didn't want to do anything. He let his fingers run over the yellow walls. He felt for the join in the paper, and picked at it, until a little rip appeared. He pulled harder.

"Whatever are you doing, Josh?"
said Mom. "You'll spoil it!"

Josh just grunted. He felt as if
everything was spoiled already.

Mom gave him a cuddle.

"Why did Max have to die, Mom?" asked Josh. "I don't want never to see him again." Fat tears began to trickle down his cheeks.

"None of us wanted this to happen, Josh," said Mom. "It's hard for everyone. It's hard for Max's family. It's hard for his friends. It's hard for everyone who knew him."

"I wish it hadn't happened," muttered Josh. He brushed away the tears and felt under his pillow, reaching for his old blanket. He hadn't used it for a long time, but now he held it to his cheek and pushed his thumb into his mouth.

"What happens when we die?" Josh whispered. "Where is Max now?"

"Well," said Mom slowly, "Max's body was so hurt that it couldn't work any more, but the things that made Max special—his kindness and friendliness, all the things that made Max who he was, which we call his spirit— have gone to be with God."

Josh tried again. "But… where's Max left his body? Where is it now?" he asked.

Mom pulled Josh to his feet.

"Come with me," she said.

Josh followed Mom into the garden. They stood by the flowerbed and looked at the bare patch of earth where the flowers stood in their jar of water.

"Do you remember when Jane's hamster died?" asked Mom. Josh nodded. He remembered it well.

They had put the little hamster in a small box, and buried him under the earth in the garden. Jane had said a prayer. Later, Jane had made a cross out of lollipop sticks, and had written Hammy on it, and put it over the place where they had buried the box.

"The same things happen when a person dies," explained Mom. "Their bodies can't feel anything because they are no longer alive."

"Will Max's body be in a box?" asked Josh, still thinking of Hammy.

Mom nodded. "The box is called a coffin," she said. "It will be buried in a graveyard or a cemetery, or else cremated and then the ashes scattered in a special place."

A gust of wind blew some rose petals into the air. Josh thought about the ashes.

"Will someone say a prayer?" asked Josh. "Yes," said Mom, "at Max's funeral."

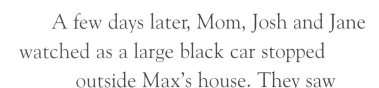

A few days later, Mom, Josh and Jane
watched as a large black car stopped
outside Max's house. They saw
Max's wife and his family get in.
"Max will be buried today,"
said Mom. "They are going to
church, to Max's funeral."
Josh half wanted to go to
Max's funeral. Mom had told
him that Max's family and
friends would sing hymns, say
prayers and ask God to look
after Max. Josh thought about
how he and Max had
decorated his bedroom.
Suddenly Josh felt very
cross. "I don't want to
go!" he said firmly.

25

Later that day, Mom, Josh and Jane walked slowly to the cemetery. They walked past the market and Mom and Jane bought a bunch of flowers. Josh chose a shiny red apple. They saw Max's wife and baby daughter. They saw his family and friends. Some of them were dressed in black, and some of them were crying.

Josh looked away.

Mom found the place where other people had brought flowers for Max. Jane put their bunch with the others. They looked very pretty.

Josh carefully put the shiny red apple among them.

"Max would like that," he thought.

Later that day, Josh lay in bed. Mom gently stroked his forehead and, after a while, went downstairs.

Josh looked at his yellow walls and the colorful parrots which went around the room.

He got out of bed.

He looked in his drawer and found the photo of Max and himself by the ladder. He found a pencil, and put it behind his ear. He reached under his bed and found a scrap of wallpaper. He arranged them all together on the floor.

Josh sat down beside them and closed his eyes.

"Dear God," he said, "thank you for Max. I wish he hadn't died. I will miss him very much. Please look after him in heaven." Josh opened his eyes. He knew that he would always remember Max. He thought about the swing and the apple tree.

Suddenly, Josh felt a lump in his throat and tears sprang up and ran down his cheeks. Alone in his bedroom, it felt good to cry.

29